PUFFI

Catfoot and the Case of the Missing Bits of
London

Alan Davidson is married with four children.
Before turning to writing books he was a
freelance writer and editor and worked
closely with Oxfam in the overseas aid field.
He first surfaced as a humorous writer with
the Annabel books, the eponymous heroine
being widely hailed as a 'female William'. His
novel, *The Bewitching of Alison Allbright* was
on the Master List 1994, South Carolina Junior
Book Award.

Other books by Alan Davidson

CATFOOT AND THE CASE OF THE BIG WOOFY DOG
CATFOOT AND THE CASE OF THE HUNTED DAD
CATFOOT AND THE CASE OF THE LAND THAT
TV FORGOT

THE BEWITCHING OF ALISON ALLBRIGHT

CATFOOT
and the case of
THE MISSING BITS OF LONDON

By Alan Davidson

Illustrated by Noel Ford

PUFFIN BOOKS

PUFFIN BOOKS

Published by the Penguin Group
Penguin Books Ltd, 27 Wrights Lane, London W8 5TZ, England
Penguin Books USA Inc., 375 Hudson Street, New York, New York 10014, USA
Penguin Books Australia Ltd, Ringwood, Victoria, Australia
Penguin Books Canada Ltd, 10 Alcorn Avenue, Toronto, Ontario, Canada M4V 3B2
Penguin Books (NZ) Ltd, 182–190 Wairau Road, Auckland 10, New Zealand

Penguin Books Ltd, Registered Offices: Harmondsworth, Middlesex, England

First published by Straw Hat 1994
Published in Puffin Books 1995
1 3 5 7 9 10 8 6 4 2

Made and printed in England by Clays Ltd, St Ives plc

Contents

The Secret Casebook
of a Private Slye

Not to be opened before the year
AD 2050

1
London in Peril
- Unofficial!

My readers are lucky. They are the first to know about some of the most astounding crimes ever committed. Crimes that went on beneath your very nose; or above your very head; but were top secret at the time.

At last I, Catullus Foot, am telling all. In these casebooks no secret will be left unrevealed. I will amaze you. I will send you to your bed with your jaw dropping from shock. Take, for instance, the case of the -

But let me begin at the beginning. A Friday evening in November. Mum, Dad and I had just been having supper in our

flat in north London. Dad had bolted his meal and shot off to his office downstairs.

I was worried about Dad. So was Mum.

"He's over-excited and silly," she said to me. "I think he may be sickening for something. Perhaps I should have a word with the doctor."

It was true that all through the meal Dad had been laughing and muttering to himself and going red in the face.

"He's working on a big case, Mum," I said. "He's always like this when he's got a big case on."

"Not as over-excited and silly as this," said Mum, firmly.

Honestly! Dad is Augustus Foot, famous as the world's greatest private eye, sometimes known as Foot of the Yard. But Mum always talks as if he's a big baby. I suppose she's right.

I went to my room. My worries weren't the same as Mum's. What bothered me was that I hadn't been able to find out what Dad's big case was about. Normally he gets excited and blabs about his cases, even when they're supposed to be secret. *Especially* when they're supposed to be secret.

But this time he'd been going around with puffed-out cheeks and hand over his mouth, saying things like "I know something you don't know". In an awed sort of voice.

That's how I knew this case was really big.

And I had to find out. Because it is I, Catullus Foot - otherwise Catfoot - who has to solve cases for him with the help of my magic catsuit. It is I who have brought him his fame.

Dad couldn't solve a baby's jigsaw

being absent-minded, unobservant and - I hate to say this because I love my Dad dearly - a bit thick. All right, a LOT thick. Though otherwise the finest Dad you could hope for which is why I make sure he gets the cred. Luckily he's so thick that he always believes he's done it himself. Which is how I like it.

No-one's ever known this. Till now.

But if I didn't know what this case was, how could I solve it?

Normally, I'm careful about wearing my catsuit around the house when Mum's in. Its magical powers are secret from everybody but especially Mum and Dad. And while Dad would never notice anything, Mum might. But this was an emergency.

The instant I put it on I felt different. I purred and had a nice stretch and a lick of my fur and a prowl round the room. It's fun being a cat. It was found by an old professor in one of the temples of Bast, the ancient Egyptian cat goddess. It's a bit tatty but what do you expect after a couple of thousand years or more?

Then I opened the window and nipped down the drainpipe. Directly below is the window to Dad's office. If I could see what he was doing that might tell me something. I hung down and peeped.

I got a shock. The curtains were drawn. Yes, I know it was dark outside and the lights were on and most people draw their curtains then. But Dad doesn't. Too much trouble.

"Fish fingers and old haddock heads!" I thought, astounded. "*Dad's attending to security!* Just how big is this case?"

With my cat's acute senses I could overhear Dad pacing up and down. He was muttering to himself.

14

"This is the big one. Yes, sir. But I'll crack it. Just leave it to Augustus Foot."

He always talks in that daft way. He thinks it makes him sound like Humphrey Bogart in old private eye films. He loves those films.

That wasn't any help.

There was another way I might see into the office. It was still riskier but I decided to take a chance. I slunk in through the back door and put my eye to the keyhole of the office door.

All I could see was office. Desk. Trench coat and Humphrey Bogart hat hanging on hook. Nothing else -

Dad suddenly came into view. He was marching straight towards me. His hand was outstretched and he was holding something between thumb and forefinger. He must be about to open the door. He'd find me. Even a cat couldn't leap out of the way quickly enough -

My view suddenly disappeared. He'd stuffed the small thing he'd been holding into the keyhole. I heard him turn away, still muttering.

"Yes, sir. The big one. But Foot of the Yard will crack it."

He'd blocked the keyhole! MORE SECURITY!

Mindblown, I hauled myself back up the drainpipe.

Could I believe my own whiskers?

In my room, I took my catsuit off. What use was a magic catsuit if Dad was going to confuse everything by behaving sensibly?

Defeated, I went back to the sitting

room where Mum was doing a crossword puzzle. Hardly was I in there when Dad flung the door open.

"I can't keep quiet any longer," he shouted. "I'm going to tell you about my case."

Phew! All you have to do with Dad is wait.

19

"I, Augustus Foot, sometimes known as Foot of the Yard, am the only person who can save London as we know it."

"Really, dear?" said Mum, chewing her pencil. "What's *A large clock.* Two words each of three letters?"

"There is a plot," yelled Dad, "to steal London's most famous monuments."

"*Big Ben*," said Mum, writing it in.

"Yes, Big Ben. Tower Bridge, perhaps… Who knows which ones?"

Mum put her pencil down and looked at him.

"Nelson's Column?" she suggested, gently. "Buckingham Palace?"

"Any of them," bawled Dad. "Maybe all of them."

Mum looked at me, sadly. She got up and took Dad's hand.

"Why would anyone want to do that, dear?" she asked, softly.

20

"I don't know," Dad shouted. "But it may be a plot to ruin Britain's tourist trade. That's why it must remain secret. Jobs may depend on this. All those people who sell picture postcards and T-shirts with messages about London on them. And plastic models of Tower Bridge..."

"Ice cream," said Mum, soothingly. "Junk food."

Dad started to cry.

"All those little people who live off the holiday trade. Ruined. And perhaps it won't only be London..."

"Will Blackpool Tower be stolen?" said Mum, stroking his hand. "The Forth Bridge?"

"Who knows?" said Dad, wiping his eyes and blowing his nose. "But I must pull myself together. Remember that I am Foot of the Yard. Tough, ruthless, cynical."

"Of course you are, dear," crooned Mum. "You frighten everybody. But how do you know all this?"

"I got a tip-off," sniffed Dad. "A letter. Sent to me. Top secret."

"Can we see it?" asked Mum.

"Of course you can." Dad felt in his pockets.

"Had it a minute ago. Must've left it in

the office. I'll get it."

He came back after a few minutes. He'd put on his trench coat, collar turned up, and Humphrey Bogart hat, pulled over one eye.

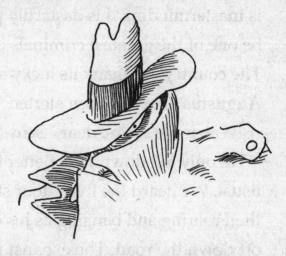

"I've lost it," he said. "But it doesn't matter. I can remember what was in it. Mostly. Anyway, I must be off. Don't expect me back till morning. I shall be guarding monuments. I have a hunch which one the villains will try first."

"Which, dear?" said Mum.

Dad put a finger along his nose, slyly.

"I can't tell you everything. But I'll give you a clue. There are pigeons around it."

He turned to go, then looked back.

"One other thing," he cried. "Whoever is masterminding this dastardly plot must be one of the greatest criminals on earth. The country can thank its lucky stars that Augustus Foot has been alerted."

"Watch the stairs, dear," said Mum.

He only fell down two. Better than usual. We heard the front door slam and then roaring and banging as his car jerked off down the road. The exhaust pipe's gone. It's a big old American car, an open Pontiac, all lights and fins like you see in old films.

"I'll ring the doctor in the morning," sighed Mum. She looked sad. She loves Dad really, like I do.

This time I didn't argue.

When I went to bed I couldn't sleep.
Poor Dad. A sick man out there in the
night guarding Nelson's Column.
Believing somebody was going to pinch it.
Fooled by some practical joker. The fame
had been too much for him. Pushed him
round the bend.

By the middle of the night I couldn't
stand it any longer. I got out of bed and
put my catsuit on. I had to go to my dad.
Look after him. What's a son for?

Especially a son with a working magic
catsuit.

2
Nelson Sails Off

I left by my usual route. The drainpipe
and a leap over the back wall. To relieve
my feelings I yowled into the night,
setting a lot of other cats off. I thought I
heard Mum shout "Getoutofit".

Then I took my catsuit off, rolled it up
tight and stuffed it inside the front of my
shirt. No point in wasting energy. I
caught an all-night bus to Trafalgar
Square.

The square was empty. Just a few
passing cars. No sign of Dad.

I didn't know what to do. I thought I
must have got it wrong. After all, there

are pigeons everywhere in London, not just round Nelson's Column. St. Paul's. The Tower. Everywhere.

I was wondering about going back home when I happened to glance at Nelson's Column and it sort of hit me between the eyes.

There were ladders up it. All the way to the top. The cleaners must be at work.

Yes. There was a contractor's board. It said:

CROOK AND MITRE CLEANING
SERVICES

SPECIALISTS IN ANCIENT
MONUMENTS

What a challenge to a cat of spirit! To go pelting all the way up those ladders. To Nelson! In one big bound!

There was nobody about. I put my catsuit on.

I don't want to make you jealous but...YOW! It was FANTASTIC. I took a deep breath and WHOOSH! I became a dark streak up the column.

And there I was suddenly, resting a paw on Nelson's plinth. He still towered above me. He's gigantic when you get up close.

But I needed a moment's rest before leaping on to his head.

Suddenly my whiskers twitched. They'd sensed something. I looked down.

"Well, blow-dry my whiskers!" I said to myself, amazed.

A beefeater was walking towards Nelson's column. Yes, a beefeater like they have at the Tower of London in that brilliant red and yellow outfit and carrying a pike over one shoulder.

GUESS WHO! →

Just then two policemen stepped from behind one of the lions.

"You are under arrest," one of them said to the beefeater. "We have been following you around London, observing your suspicious behaviour."

"Under arrest!" gasped the beefeater. "On what charge?"

I knew that voice! It was Dad!

"Four charges, sir. Disorderly conduct; suspicion of theft of one beefeater's outfit; possession of an offensive weapon, namely, a pike; and driving a motor vehicle on a public road with a defective exhaust pipe."

"I have not been disorderly," gasped Dad.

"Then why, sir, have you been running around London frightening people? Several innocent citizens have taken you to be a nightmare."

"Very well," said Dad. "Since you are the police I will explain. I am here on a secret mission to defend Nelson's Column from a criminal mastermind who intends to steal it. The costume is a disguise so that I will remain inconspicuous. I hired it from a theatrical outfitters. Now do you understand?"

"It's the poorest alibi I've heard for some time," said the policeman, shaking his head while making notes.

"For a start," said the second policeman, "beefeaters' outfits are worn at the Tower of London, not Nelson's Column."

"Silly me!" gasped Dad, clapping his hand to his head. "I've been so silly all night. First I went to Billingsgate where that other tall column is - "

"I'd like you to come with us, sir," said the first policeman, kindly. "You will be

32

well looked after, TV and your own washbasin in every room. I assure you, sir, that Nelson is quite safe. He would be very difficult to steal."

I leaned forward to get a better look. As I did so I pushed against Nelson's plinth.

Nelson fell off his column.

Yes, I say again in case you didn't catch it first time. Nelson fell off his column. Complete with plinth.

My whiskers stiffened in horror. What had I done?

CATastrophic.

Then I saw that Nelson was just sort of sinking slowly. Also, he was staying the right way up, like a balloon with weights in the bottom.

It wasn't the real Nelson at all! Just a copy made of lightweight plastic that had been glued to the top of the column.

The real Nelson had gone.

I knew that I was witnessing something unique in history; something the like of which might never be seen again. Yes.

DAD HADN'T BEEN TALKING GIBBERISH. HE'D BEEN RIGHT ALL ALONG.

And as if that weren't enough for one day, Nelson had been pinched and a cheap plastic copy left in his place.

By whom?

Then I noticed something gleaming by my paws. I picked it up. A chess piece made of gold. A bishop. Something stirred in my memory.

From below came shouts of amazement. The plastic Nelson settled beside Dad, towering over him and facing the two policemen. It was as if he'd come to Dad's help.

"You see," shouted Dad, triumphantly, clapping Nelson's plinth. "This isn't the real Nelson, is it. Even Scotland Yard would admit that. The real Nelson's been stolen and this shoddy imitation left in its place. It's so shoddy the glue's come unstuck."

It was one of the big moments of Dad's life. The policemen were open-mouthed. Dad waved his pike.

"Next time Foot of the Yard tells you something, perhaps you'll believe it," he yelled. "I suggest you do because that way lies promotion."

"Foot of the Yard!" gasped the first policeman. "You mean - you're Foot of the Yard." They both snapped to attention. "Why didn't you say so, sir?"

"Your name is a legend in the Metropolitan Police," said the other. "We often talk about you on patrol. But we never expected to have the privilege of meeting you."

They saluted. Dad clanked his pike on Trafalgar Square.

"But who is behind this, sir?" said the first policeman. "What villain is big enough to mastermind the theft of Nelson without anyone knowing?"

I thought I'd give them a helping paw. I threw down the golden chess piece. It fell at the feet of the first policeman and he picked it up.

"And here's the answer," he gasped.
"Look what's fallen off the column. Left
here by - "

"The Bishop!" cried the other
policeman, in awe.

Yes, I'd remembered.

The Bishop. The world's greatest
criminal. From his palatial headquarters
in Switzerland he ran a vast international
network of crime. No job was too big for
him. No country was safe. No police force

could cope. He had his own private air force of jet planes and helicopters. Even, it was murmured, his own spy satellite.

No-one knew his true identity. There were rumours that he was a top statesman, a famous film star, a member of some royal family, perhaps even a real bishop. But they were only rumours. Sometimes, photographs of him were published. But always masked, dressed as a bishop with crook and mitre.

The bishop was known to like his little joke. That was why, wherever in the world his men operated, somewhere on the job they left behind his 'calling card', a golden chess piece. A bishop.

This, then, was the man known as the Archbishop of Crime. The mastermind who could steal Nelson from his column. And, for all I knew, might pinch Buckingham Palace as well. Who could

cope with him?

Below me, Dad shook his pike at the sky.

"At last," he screamed. "A challenge worthy of me. A clash of Titans. The Bishop versus Foot of the Yard. Seldom has the world seen the like. And only one shall prevail!"

I slid thoughtfully down the ladders, hidden by the column.

I had a big job on my paws.

Also, I'd had a thought about that tip-off of Dad's.

3
A Load of
Plastic Rubbish

I skulked behind a lion for a last listen.

"Now I hope you policemen won't get in the way while I'm investigating," Dad was shouting. "You mean well but you know the reputation Scotland Yard has for making a mess of things. Every private eye since Sherlock Holmes has had this problem."

"Yes, Mr Foot," replied the first policeman, humbly. "We know our place. We will do the dirty work, of course, tidy up afterwards. But since you're on the case we know the Commissioner will be leaving the brainwork to you."

I took my catsuit off and caught a bus home. I sneaked in quietly so as not to wake Mum and went straight to Dad's office. From his keyhole I fished out the thing I'd seen him push in there.

It was a tightly folded piece of paper. I opened it out.

Yes, it was the tip-off. Dad had used it to block the keyhole. It was handwritten with no address or date.

To Foot of the Yard. TOP SECRET.

Dear Mr Foot

I am risking my life to send this. But I know I can rely on you. I've read in the papers that you are the greatest private eye in the world. I dare not go to the police.

I am a criminal, Mr Foot. I am what is known in the trade as a bent steeplejack. I specialise in stealing from great heights. I have been offered big money to help steal London's most famous monuments. Nelson's Column, Eros, that sort of thing. They are to be sold to a foreign power which wants them for its own tourist industry. Some Mr Big is behind this. Some Mr VERY Big.

I may be a crook, Mr Foot, but I am a British crook and a patriot. This is not right and I will have nothing to do with it. No foreign power should be allowed to nick our heritage. But I know our monuments will be safe in your hands.

For our beloved monarch and country!

A PATRIOT

There might be a clue on the envelope.
Where was it? Dad's office door was
unlocked. He'd given up attending to
security. I switched on the light.

Waste paper basket. That was where
clues usually got put. I poked through it.
Banana skins, old doodles - self portraits
of Dad with *The Greatest* written
underneath. Here it was, a screwed-up
envelope. I unscrewed it. Brazilian stamp.
Postmarked *Rio de Janeiro*. No other clue.

I heard banging and roaring up the

street. Dad was coming back. I went to bed.

To sleep...to sleep perchance to dream. Perhaps to nightmare. I dreamed I was in my catsuit. I was pelting across the roof of the Houses of Parliament pursued by a fighter aircraft firing rockets at me. I shot up the tower of Big Ben and as I did so the hour started booming. I clung to the minute hand in terror, wrapping my tail round it. The plane was coming straight

at me. The pilot smirked as he fired again. He was masked and wore one of those Bishop's hats they call a mitre... He waved his crook out of the window.

I woke up, yowling with defiance.

When I turned on my bedside radio in the morning, I expected to hear about Nelson on the news. But not a cheep. At breakfast I found out why.

"It's a secret," yelled Dad, when he'd finished telling Mum and me about how Nelson had been pinched and he, Dad, had discovered it. "The police have put the dummy Nelson back on its column so no-one will know."

"If it's a secret," said Mum, "you'd better close the window. But why is it a secret?"

"We will not let those villains ruin the tourist trade," roared Dad. "That's what

46

they want. We won't have tourists
disappointed by seeing Nelson's Column
with nothing on top."

"You're so wise, dear," nodded Mum.
"Now I'd like you to have a word with the
doctor. Just a little check-up. When's a
good time?"

"Foot of the Yard has no time to bother
with his own health. The country needs
me. I'm going back to bed. Tonight I shall
be out defending monuments again and
this time I'll be ready for the villains."

I couldn't tell Mum that Dad was
RIGHT for once.

"All right," she sighed. "Well, I shan't
see you till tomorrow. I'm going to Nanny
and Grandpa's. I'll be staying the night."

Mum's parents live in Brighton. She
goes there often. You can't blame her.
After she'd gone, I went to bed, too.
Luckily it was Saturday. Dad's snores

were already shaking the house.

I also had work to do that night. Something Dad hadn't thought of. Naturally.

At midnight I heard Dad's car bang off again. I got up and caught a bus to town. It was a damp, dark, misty night.

I was going to check monuments. If the Bishop had pinched Nelson he might already have got others.

I started with Cleopatra's Needle, on the Thames Embankment. It just happened to be the first one I thought of. There was a bit of scaffolding round it and a contractor's sign, the same one as at Nelson's Column. More cleaning work.

I was like a doctor with a patient. I got into my catsuit, as if it were a surgeon's gown, nipped up the Needle, tapped it with the knuckle of my paw, listened.

It hurt my paw. Good, solid granite.

48

Anyway, Cleopatra's Needle had been a daft idea. What next?

I decided to get organised and work from west to east. I got a bus to Kensington Gardens and started with Peter Pan. Catsuit on again. Shin up plinth. Tap.

Like tapping an empty margarine tub.
Peter Pan was fake. So was his nice
plinth.

I kept my catsuit on and loped across
London checking more. Of the twenty-
five I checked, twenty-three were fakes.
Only Eros and the Duke of York were
real. Plus Cleopatra's Needle, of course.

Among the fakes were Richard the
Lionheart, Queen Victoria, the Duke of
Wellington and Marble Arch. Albert had
been pinched out of the Albert Memorial.

The Duke of York was the last one I
checked. He's on top of a tall column just
off the Mall. I enjoyed scooting up him,
especially when I found he was real. He
was as good a scoot as Nelson's Column.

After that I gave up. More checking
seemed pointless. Almost everything
worth pinching was already gone. Dad
was guarding a load of plastic rubbish.

I sat under Admiralty Arch out of the drizzle and licked my chops. What could I do? This was a national emergency and I was only a cat. A clever cat. But a cat. Could I really save the situation and give Dad the cred? Was it possible?

It was four in the morning, a time when a cat should be at its best. I felt low. I scratched. Maybe I was getting fleas as well.

I tried to get into the Bishop's mind. Supposing I had all those aeroplanes and helicopters to play with. How would I pinch a monument?

Well, I thought, I'd get fake workmen to pretend to be cleaning it. They'd loosen it, ready for snatching. Then I'd choose a damp, dark, misty night when nobody's about and I'd stage an accident. Something that'd get all the police cars rushing to it, away from the monument -

What was that?

A police siren. Coming towards me from the Embankment. In the distance I heard others.

It was a damp, dark, misty night. Nobody was about. I remembered that contractor's sign... The same as at Nelson's Column...

"Dustbins and rooftops!" I breathed. "Crook and Mitre Cleaning Services!"

Who but a Bishop had a crook and mitre? One of the Bishop's little jokes.

I moved like a scalded cat. Cleopatra's Needle was being pinched under my very whiskers.

4
Dad Makes a Splash

The police car howled past as I shot by
Trafalgar Square, going the other way.
They were too busy to see me. Then I was
streaking towards the river. How long
did it take the Bishop to pinch a
monument?

I turned left along the Embankment,
underneath the railway bridge…

I could see the Needle. It was still there.
I slowed…

I saw a movement. I hissed and sprang
forward again. I needed a better view. I
climbed the Needle in a bound.

As I did so, it bent. The tip twisted over.

It was another plastic fake. They'd pinched the real one while I'd been roaming around London.

And from where I was now, I could see it!

It was lying along the deck of a long, low boat that was just moving away from the sort of jetty which sticks out into the

river there.

There was a crane on the boat. They'd
raised it to lift the Needle off. Now it was
being lowered again, like a jack-knife
blade. It was that that I'd seen moving. It
came to rest beside the Needle. There was
nobody on deck. The crew must be in the
wheelhouse forward.

I wanted to leap aboard but already it was too far away, even for a cat like me.

Suddenly, with a deep throb, the boat surged forward. It must have had a terrifically powerful engine.

I almost fell down the fake Needle. How could I get aboard? Find out where it was going? I pelted along the Embankment in pursuit. I became a dark blur.

The only hope was to get ahead of it and drop on to it from a bridge. Risk being seen. But already it was moving under Waterloo Bridge and I was tiring. Even a cat has its limits. The next bridge was Blackfriars.

It was Blackfriars or nothing. After that I'd be rolling over with my paws in the air.

I was overhauling the boat. Tired or not I was still moving like a Derby winner. A man walking towards me saw me coming, screamed and fled across the road. He wouldn't be going for night walks again. I was moving ahead of the boat now. Just. I raced on to Blackfriars Bridge. It was coming up to the central arch.

I leapt over the rail, touching it lightly with my paws, and on to the narrow ledge below. The boat was directly beneath me, fast disappearing under the bridge. I didn't hesitate. It was now or never. I dropped.

My fur stood on end. Only the teeniest bit of stern still showed, followed by a wake of churning water. If I missed…you know how we cats feel about water.

I sort of bicycled and twisted in the air, flung out a paw and clung. I just managed to catch the stern rail by the skin of a whisker. For a moment I streamed out behind the boat, gripping with my claws,

57

then I crawled on to the deck and hid under the end of the crane.

I waited, heaving, wondering if I'd been seen.

Nobody came. After a minute I relaxed and took my catsuit off and stuffed it inside my shirt. If I were caught, better to look like a harmless kid.

I'd recovered now and a feeling of warm satisfaction came over me. I'd made a breakthrough. I was on my way to finding the stolen monuments. Now, suddenly, I knew I could crack this case for Dad. With my catsuit, nothing could stop me. Absolutely nothing.

I poked my head out and looked around. We'd just passed under London Bridge. Tower Bridge, the last one, lay ahead. How far were we going?

Hold it, though. Something funny was going on. A guardsman was marching up and down Tower Bridge. I could see the scarlet tunic, the black busby, the rifle. First one way, stamp, stamp, stamp, then back again...

What was a guardsman doing on Tower Bridge? Guardsmen guarded palaces, not bridges. Had he made a mistake. No guardsman would be so daft...

Who *would* be so daft? Nobody. Except...

Well, if it *was* Dad, at least he couldn't do any harm there. Probably the best place for him, safely out of the way.

A ship's siren suddenly boomed ahead. The bascules of Tower Bridge started to lift. They were opening for a ship. They hardly ever open nowadays but -

Dad never has any luck!

He was doing a smart about turn when the bridge parted beneath him. He

GUESS WHO
- AGAIN?

smacked his rifle butt hard, stamped twice
into air and shot downwards.

We were just coming up to the bridge at
the time and he hit the water right beside
us. It was a big splash. Army boots are
heavy. He disappeared below the surface
then shot up again on the bounce.

I couldn't let my dad drown. I leapt
from hiding, snatched a lifebelt and rope
and flung them to him. He grabbed the
rope just as he was going under again,
came up spluttering for the second time
and managed to get the lifebelt on.

He didn't know who was rescuing him.
I don't suppose it mattered. I started
hauling.

The rope was suddenly snatched from
me by a man snarling "Hold him". He was
a huge man with a broken nose, a real
thug. Somebody else seized me from
behind and pulled me away. The big man
hauled twice as fast as I did and Dad
came catapulting over the rail like a fish.

He fell on the deck in a squelchy heap,
still clinging to his rifle, busby over one
eye. Then he jumped to his feet.

"You will be richly rewarded for this,"
he cried. He was steadying himself by

holding on to Cleopatra's Needle. "Know that it is no ordinary person you have saved but Foot of the Yard. I am engaged in preventing the Bishop's men from stealing London's priceless monuments. I shall recommend you for a medal."

I was out of sight behind the crane, helpless. Dad suddenly realised what he was leaning against.

"Cleopatra's Needle!" he gasped.

He drew back his shoulders and straightened his busby. Water poured from it and down his face.

"You are the Bishop's men!" he shouted. "I knew I'd track you down. You see? You are no match for Foot of the Yard. I arrest you in the name of - "

"Throw him back!" snarled the big man to two other men who'd appeared. "It's Footy."

"Right you are, Big Nige," said one of them. Big Nige was obviously in command. Perhaps he was the Bishop's right hand man.

They threw him in again. Also his rifle, which floated. It was wooden. Luckily, they hadn't taken his lifebelt off; an oversight, probably. So he ought to be all right. He'd popped up just long enough to ruin things, as usual.

"And who are you?" snarled Big Nige, turning to me. He always snarled.

"My name's Eric Smith, sir," I said innocently. I was watching Dad thrashing towards the river bank, getting out of the way of the big ship. "I missed my bus home and had nowhere to sleep. So I crept on your boat."

He stared hard. I didn't look much of a threat.

"Put him in a cabin," he snarled to the man holding me. "And give him some cocoa to help him sleep."

The cocoa must have had knock-out drops in it because I went out like a light. When I woke up I was no longer on a boat. I was lying on a mattress thrown on the floor of an unfurnished room.

I sat up. It looked like a swish modern office with a connecting cloakroom.

I got up and tried the door. Locked. I went to the window. A small ventilator in the top opened out. I stuck my head out and looked down. Dawn was breaking.

I was high up in what looked to be a huge empty office block. Way below me I could see a big garden completely surrounded by more office blocks. Trees and shrubs in the garden were bathed in a soft glow. It was peculiar.

A normal person would be completely trapped up here.

Normal person, hah!

I got into my catsuit and squeezed myself through the ventilator. Then, dropping from window sill to window sill, I went down into the garden.

And there I crouched in amazement. I was in a fantastic world.

5
In the Garden
of Stolen Heritage

It was more like a park than a garden.
There were trees and fountains and shady
nooks and hidden lights giving that glow.

But what made it weird were the
monuments. Richard the Lionheart
waved his sword at me from the
rhododendrons. Shakespeare eyed me
across a fountain. Huge in a clearing was
Marble Arch. In the next clearing was
Nelson.

Winston Churchill, Florence
Nightingale, Queen Victoria, Peter
Pan...dozens of them. I prowled amongst
them, eyes popping. All London's stolen

CHURCHILL

monuments had been hidden here.

And what a place to hide them,
completely concealed by empty office
blocks! I needed to get out, raise the
alarm, somehow make sure Dad got the

cred. I slunk around looking for a way of escape.

There were only two exits, both through archways. Both were guarded.

One archway led to what must be the street. At the far end I could see steel gates and guards. The other led to the river. I could see more guards lurking there on a wharf. I guessed I was in a Docklands development with all the offices waiting to be let. And I was trapped.

I was wondering what to do when I heard voices. I knew that snarl. I slunk nearer and shinned up a tree for a better view. I padded out along a branch and almost bumped into Cleopatra's Needle.

It was now standing upright among the trees and at the foot of it, almost directly below me, was Big Nige. With him was another man. This man wore a leather jacket, his hands were deep in his pockets and he was yawning.

"Only two more monuments to nick," Big Nige was saying. He was ticking

things off in a notebook, licking his pencil. "Eros and the Dook of York. We'll get 'em tonight if conditions are right and that'll wrap the job up."

"I'll start getting this lot aboard, then," said the other man, looking around, still yawning. "It'll take time. Non-stop work, this is. Haven't had a proper sleep for days. Lucky the pay's good."

"The best," said Big Nige. "Nobody pays better than the Bishop. So get on with it. Load everyfink today. Eros and the Dook can be dropped straight on to the ship. Sail at dawn tomorrow."

"Twenty-four hours!" I thought, licking my chops. "I've only got twenty-four hours to save London. Still, that ought to be enough for a resourceful cat like me."

"I'm going to take a look at that kid," Big Nige was saying. "He seems harmless but I can't be certain."

He meant me. I slid out of the tree.

I was back on the mattress, catsuit off, when Big Nige came in. No point in alarming anybody. Yet.

"Will anyone be missing you at home?" he asked, trying to put charm into his snarl.

"Mum and Dad will," I said, innocently. "Can I go now?"

"Not yet." He went to the ventilator. I'd left it open. "Have you been looking out?"

"Just getting some fresh air," I said, still innocent.

He shut it, turned a little screw and took it off, putting it in his pocket. He'd locked it. Now I was properly trapped. I began to hope twenty-four hours really was long enough.

At eight o'clock a man brought me some breakfast on a tray. Cornflakes. Toast. Butter. Marmalade. Tea. It was better than nothing. And at eleven o'clock Big Nige came back with a mobile phone.

"Ring home," he snarled, forgetting the charm. "Make an excuse. If you're not convincing you'll never get out of here. I'll be listening."

"Yes, sir," I said, meekly.

Mum answered the phone.

"I came back first thing this morning,"

she said. "I was worried about Dad. Where are you, Catullus? I thought you were in bed."

She didn't sound worried now. No more than was normal, anyway. So Dad must be all right.

"At Charlie's," I said, one eye on Big Nige. Charlie's my friend. I stay with him often though not as often as Mum thinks. "We're going to the pictures this evening and his Mum's invited me to stay the night again. How's Dad?"

"He came in half an hour ago. Sopping wet in a guardsman's uniform. Said his car's broken down and he didn't have any money to get home with. Lost it all in the river or something and had to walk all the way from Tower Bridge. I don't know what he's been up to. It's a scream, really. He's in a real tiz because he says all London's monuments have been stolen now. I still can't get him to a doctor."

So the police must have checked the monuments, too. And they'd have told Dad.

"Says the police are baffled and relying on him to get them back. He's out right now having a model of Eros made. Don't know why. Urgent, he says. You have to laugh. Now remember you've got school tomorrow, Catullus. No staying up late with Charlie tonight."

I couldn't say anything more. Big Nige's hand was hovering nearby, waiting to snatch the phone if I made a wrong move. I said goodbye and handed it back to him.

"When will you let me go?" I asked, still meek.

"That's not up to me," he snarled and left, taking the phone with him.

Who *was* it up to? I wondered. And why was Dad having a model of Eros made?

For the time being I was helpless as a new born kitten. Also dog tired (to use a phrase I don't care for). Since I could do nothing else, I slept. I just had to hope something would happen to break the deadlock. It was Sunday.

I slept on and off for most of the day, feeling I had to keep my strength up. For what, though? Apart from being brought meals, nothing happened. By midnight I was a cat on hot bricks, even without my catsuit on. What was I going to do?

It was just before three in the morning when the door was throw open by Big Nige.

"Get up and follow me," he snarled.

I was so grateful for anything happening that I could have purred. But where was he taking me?

"You'll see," he snarled, when I asked him.

I followed him down some stairs to a landing. There he opened a door and pushed me through it. The door closed behind me.

I was outside in the dark, dank, misty night; high up above the streets on a big flat concrete platform. The lights of London glowed faintly all round into the distance. Below me was the river and the masts of a ship, probably the one with the monuments aboard. Lights on the platform pointed upwards to the sky.

I was on a helicopter pad! And then, as my eyes became accustomed to the darkness I saw something else.

A man was looking at me from the pool of darkness in the middle of the pad. Behind him towered two statues. They were Eros and the Duke of York. Or maybe they were plastic copies.

The man was dressed in robes and mitre and held a bishop's crook in his hand. He was masked.

I was alone with the most powerful criminal in the world.

6
Little Jokes
with the Bishop

"Come closer," ordered the Bishop.

He had a smooth, deep voice. He might have been about to give a sermon.

I did so. I stood meekly in front of him and he ran his eye over me from top to toe. So intently that I thought he might prod me. I was being checked out by the one man who could order my release.

He seemed satisfied with what he saw.

"I am sorry to have had to keep you here," he said, at last. His voice was relaxed. He must have decided I was harmless. "Nigel is efficient but he is not good company. He snarls too much."

"He doesn't have any little jokes, sir," I said, feeling my way. I was hoping he was going to let me go.

"Exactly." A sort of booming chuckle started in his throat. "I can see you are a boy after my own heart. I see no reason why you should not be released after a few days."

A few days! Leftover codsheads! That wasn't any good.

"What are these statues for?" I asked, looking wide-eyed, playing the innocent. I was trying to think what to do.

My interest pleased him. Again that chuckle. He patted my head, just as if he were blessing me.

"Since you're such a nice boy I'll let you into a secret. They're not real statues. Look."

He poked the Duke of York with a finger. The Duke wobbled.

"You see? Plastic. Hollow as an empty orange juice bottle." His laugh became gleeful, almost a giggle. The Bishop obviously liked to show off. He was warming up. "It's most amusing. I am stealing London's most priceless monuments and replacing them with rubbish. Don't you think that's an excellent little joke?"

"That's very funny," I laughed. "What will you do with them, sir?"

"The real ones will go to Punia where President Ghastli is building a new capital, Ghastliville. The monuments - you'll like this - are to be put in a theme park there." The Bishop's shoulders shook.

I started rolling around and holding my sides. "So all the tourists," I gasped, "will go to Punia instead of London."

"Exactly. As soon as it is safe to do so I

82

shall tell the world that London's monuments are all plastic. Junk. I shall enjoy that."

"Enough to make a cat laugh," I hooted. I almost clapped him on the shoulder.

"An even bigger joke - listen to this - is that an idiot called Foot of the Yard is trying to stop me. I call him Fool of the Yard. Ha ha ha."

I didn't like that one so much but I didn't show it. He patted me on the head again. From somewhere above I heard the throb of a helicopter coming closer.

"Since we are getting on so well together," he said, "I shall give you a little present when I free you. An air ticket to Ghastliville to see the theme park."

"Oh, thank you, sir," I said. I looked at the Duke of York. "I can't really believe that's hollow, though. It's so real. I think you're having me on. You're making it all

83

up. You're having another little joke."

"I'll show you," said the Bishop. "It's possible to get inside him. Watch."

He pressed something and a panel in the back of the Duke of York's cloak and leg swung open. The helicopter noise was getting closer.

"Neat, is it not?" said the Bishop. "It was necessary to get inside to make them. I have a factory producing plastic monuments in this very building."

"You're brilliant, sir," I breathed. "You ought to be up on top of that column, a great man, not that silly old Duke of York."

"I agree with you," he said. His shoulders were heaving again. But I'd be too small as I am. The Duke's so much bigger than me."

I was laughing again, too. We really did get on like a house on fire. "Perhaps you

should get inside him," I suggested. "*Then* you'd be big."

"Like this?" he said, still laughing, and stepped inside the Duke of York. I was still laughing too as I slammed the panel shut.

I didn't know if it could be opened from the inside and I didn't wait to find out. In the flick of a whisker I had my catsuit out, was into it and skidding down the longest drainpipe of my cat's career.

I hit the pavement and fled. The helicopter was hovering right overhead now. Gigantic office blocks towered around. I guessed I was on the Isle of Dogs (a silly name, I always think).

At full pelt I came to a main road and

saw a traffic sign. I turned left towards
the West End, heading for Piccadilly
Circus and Eros. I guessed Dad might be
up to something there. He wasn't having
that model of Eros made for nothing. And
Eros was next for pinching.

I sneaked a lift on a passing van bumper
then another on the back of a lorry that

took me to Trafalgar Square. I streaked up the Haymarket so fast that I almost knocked a pedestrian over. He screamed and fled. I was getting used to screaming, fleeing pedestrians. I heard a helicopter throbbing in the mists above me and put on still more speed. I saw Eros ahead.

There was something funny about Eros and it wasn't just the hoarding round him. I couldn't put my paw on it for a moment. Then I realised what it was.

He was too big. Eros himself is quite small, really. Only his plinth gives him height. I couldn't understand it. I stopped for a second to gape, sat down, licked my chops, smoothed my whiskers.

Suddenly Eros moved. His head swung back on a hinge. Another head popped out.

This other head wore a Humphrey Bogart hat.

It was Dad's head.

"You'll get a shock, you villains," he roared at the sky. "Foot of the Yard is ready and waiting for you. With handcuffs."

His head disappeared and a fist came out holding some handcuffs. It gave them a vigorous shake then that disappeared, too. The Eros head fell shut again.

So now I knew why he'd had a fake Eros made. So that he could hide inside it. The real Eros must have been moved to a place of safety.

I needed to think but I wasn't given time. Before I could so much as twitch a whisker, a noosed cable with a man clinging to it shot down from the mist above. The helicopter noise was now directly overhead. The man dropped the noose round the fake Eros then tugged on the rope.

Eros and plinth, with Dad inside, rose into the air.

Almost instantly, its place was taken by another fake Eros which came dropping out of the mist. This must be the one I'd seen on the helicopter pad. A second man on another cable guided it into place.

I wasn't staying to watch. This was all happening in the blink of an eye but even so, I was up to the challenge. I was rising up into the mists over London. I'd grabbed the plinth with my claws and was hanging on.

What's a magic catsuit for if not to help you look after your dad?

7
Flying High with Eros

It was, though, enough to make a cat spit.
Even a well brought-up cat like me.

After all the trouble I'd gone through to
escape from the Bishop and get across
London. And now I was being carried all
the way back again. Helpless!

The Augustus Foot Detective Agency
was at another of its low points. Its Chief
Investigator was dangling above London
trapped in a plastic model of Eros with its
head stuck shut. I knew it was stuck shut
because I could hear Dad shouting about
it.

"What's going on, you villains?"he was

yelling. "You poor fools! Think you can
steal Eros, eh? Just wait till I get this head
open. You'll all be under arrest."

That sort of stuff. He didn't seem to
know he was a thousand feet up in the
mist.

At the same time the agency's junior
staff was clinging on to same by the
claws. Painfully. *Very* painfully. Tail

streaming out in the breeze. It was also chilly. *Very* chilly. As always at low points, I thought of Mum. She doesn't know half of what her family gets up to when she's not looking.

Suddenly I heard a yell of terror. I looked up. The Eros head had unstuck and Dad's head had popped out again. He'd seen where he was. His Humphrey Bogart hat flew off and something fell from under it.

DAD NEVER COULD KEEP ANYTHING UNDER HIS HAT

His mobile phone. Dad sometimes keeps it under his hat for emergencies. I caught it. No point in losing a good phone even if the agency was doomed. But now I could only grip the plinth with one paw. The pain was even greater. The Eros head snapped shut again. Dad never did like heights. I suppose he didn't want to look.

But, anyway, this *was* an emergency. Maybe, I thought, I should use the phone and dial 999. I hated admitting defeat but was there any other way out...? There comes a time when you have to face facts...

I'm a practical sort of cat. I switched the phone on. I was about to dial -

That was peculiar. A voice was coming out of the phone. Or, should I say, a snarl.

It was a snarl I knew but didn't love. It was saying:

" - an emergency. The Bishop's disappeared."

Big Nige!

"Where did you see him last?" Another voice, very close.

The helicopter pilot! I realised what was happening. I was picking up a call from Big Nige to the helicopter pilot.

"On the helicopter pad with that kid." Big Nige again. "The kid's disappeared as well."

He was talking about me.

"Well, I don't know where he is," the helicopter pilot was saying. "I've got my hands full carting Eros around. These monuments aren't easy, you know."

Suddenly, I wanted to laugh. And if my left paw hadn't been killing me I would have done. I wanted to roll around kicking my paws in the air and mewing. Because I'd realised something brilliant.

I spoke. I used Dad's voice. "Listen, Big Nige," I said. "Can you hear me?"

There was a dumbfounded silence.
Then Big Nige said: "'Oo's that?"

"Foot of the Yard," I sneered. "The
world's greatest private eye." (I had to
stay in character). "You're finished, Big
Nige. Through. So is the Bishop. Nobody
crosses Foot of the Yard and gets away
with it. I've been one step ahead of you all
the way."

It was fun being Dad. Almost made me

97

forget the pain. Almost.

"What are you talking about, Footy?"

"I know where the Bishop is, Big Nige. And I'm the only person who does. Obey my orders or you'll never see him again except at prison visiting times. I can hand him over to the police or to you. The choice is yours, Big Nige. Choose."

"You're kidding, Footy. You know nothing about anything."

"Oh yeah?" My snarl was better than his snarl. "I know exactly where you've been keeping the monuments. Queen Victoria was in the herb garden. Cromwell was by the goldfish pond. Now they're aboard that ship of yours."

That rocked him. You could hear the gear-change. I put the claw in.

"I hear the Bishop's a good payer, Big Nige. But has he paid you yet?"

It was the helicopter pilot who

answered. He sort of squawked. "No, he hasn't. That's right, he hasn't, Big Nige."

"Well, if you want to see your money you'd better get him back. And that means doing what I say."

My whiskers were stiff with the strain. I couldn't hold on much longer.

"What's your price, Footy?" Big Nige was a broken man.

"I want every monument put back and the fakes taken away. Tonight. By dawn." My claw was slipping off the plinth.

"That's impossible." He was pleading now. "Be reasonable, Footy."

"Impossible?" I jeered. "What sort of crummy, small-time organisation am I dealing with? I'm used to the big time. Your boss is heading for disaster and so are you and all you can do is quibble. Wake up, Big Nige."

"Yeah," said the helicopter pilot. "Wake

up, Big Nige. I got a family to support."

"All right, all right. Tell me where the Bishop is."

"I'll tell you that," I said, "when the monuments are back in place. You don't have any choice, Big Nige. And there's another little thing I've got to tell you."

"What now?"

"That Eros your helicopter is toting around. It's a fake. Get the pilot to look. It's far too big for the real thing. That's in police custody. You're so sloppy, Big Nige."

I kept out of sight. I heard a groan from the pilot.

"He's right, Big Nige."

"I want it set down now. Instantly. Also gently." My eyes were shut tight from pain. "Give me your phone number, Big Nige, and I'll ring you back when I'm sure the monuments are all where they should be. And…one other thing…"

"Yeah?"

"Less of the Footy. It's Foot of the Yard to you."

"It's a bit of a mouthful."

"No grumbling."

"All right. Foot of the Yard."

A truly broken man.

There hadn't been a cheep out of Dad. Maybe the head was stuck again. That was just as well.

I have to say that I'd been a bit rough on Big Nige. He was really efficient. As I watched from the ground, the air above London became thick with helicopters, all

with monuments or fake monuments
hanging from them. I got glimpses of
them through the mist and I could hear
them all the time.

A few mistakes were made. Florence
Nightingale landed up in the Albert
Memorial. Shakespeare was put down
back to front. Little things like that. But it
was a great effort and, anyway, the
police got it all sorted out before anyone
noticed. I'd given them a quick call
pretending to be Dad and explaining the
situation. Or part-explaining the

situation. When Foot of the Yard spoke, they jumped.

We'd been put down in south London, just outside an underground station which was lucky because it meant I knew where I was. I had to leave Dad inside the plaster Eros. I couldn't risk being seen by him and, anyway, he was best kept out of the way for the time being. Luckily, the Eros head was still stuck.

I scooted westwards, still in my catsuit, taking the phone with me. I went straight to the Duke of York's column then sat and waited at the foot of it, listening to the helicopters thrashing about above. It was still very dark and misty. I looked up.

Was it the real Duke up there? Or a plastic one? I thought I knew but I couldn't be certain. I could have nipped up and had a look but I wasn't in any hurry.

After a while the helicopters quietened

down… I rang Big Nige.

"Is everything back yet?" I asked him.

"Everything but the Dook of York," he snarled. "That's on its way now." His snarl was back on form again. He sounded bitter. Big Nige was not a man at ease with himself.

So it *was* the plastic fake up there. Just as I'd thought. They'd have pinched the real Duke at the same time as Eros.

I saw something scudding towards me through the mist. It was the Duke of York dangling from a helicopter.

"Tell your pilot to be careful," I said to Big Nige.

"Why?"

I heard a strange sound from above. Like a margarine tub cracking into pieces. I looked up.

The plastic Duke of York was toppling from his column. Slowly, just as Nelson had. But a chunk of him was missing. It had broken off in bits which were falling separately. I had to dodge as they clattered to the ground. But as the plastic Duke sank downwards I saw that someone was left behind, on top of the column.

He crouched in terror, high above London in the darkness and mist, a masked figure in robes and mitre. In one hand he held a crook, in the other a chunk of plastic.

The Bishop.

He'd broken out at last. He'd probably been trying for a long time, beating at the plastic with his crook.

Then, suddenly, as I watched, he hurled the plastic away from him. It went skimming towards the Mall like a flat pebble that someone had thrown at the sea. He stood up straight and tall,

shoulders back. He raised his fists and
shook them in defiant triumph at the sky.

He was lording it over London like a
real monument.

A BIG crook, the Bishop.

And he liked his little joke.

"I think your pilot can see for himself," I
said to Big Nige.

It made a stir in the papers. The
helicopter activity was thought to be
some secret R.A.F. exercise. There were
quite a lot of complaints about the noise
and letters from people saying they'd seen
UFOs.

The really big news, though, was about
how a second Eros had appeared outside
the Elephant and Castle underground
station. That was where Dad and I had
been put down.

Fortunately, it was screened off by the
police before the photographers could get

there. So they didn't see it opened up in the presence of the Commissioner of the Metropolitan Police.

When Dad's head popped out the Commissioner saluted stiffly, his cane under his arm.

"Congratulations, sir," he said.

"Thank you," gasped Dad. "For anything special or just generally?"

"For saving London from that fiend the Bishop," replied the Commissioner, quietly. "We ourselves could never have done it. But, alas, the nation will never know the full story of your genius and courage."

"Can't we tell them?" asked Dad.

"The government insists we must not alarm the tourist trade," said the Commissioner. "The Prime Minister's appreciation for what you have done will be shown by a small dinner in your

honour, given by some Very Eminent
Persons. Mrs Foot will be invited to the
Palace, too. I wish we could do more."

"We heroes are used to ingratitude,"
said Dad.

The Commissioner stepped back and

saluted again. His hand quivered and
went on quivering for a full minute.

"I am deeply honoured," he said, "to
salute the first man ever to have sent the
Bishop packing with his tail between his
legs."

Which was exactly where mine was. I was observing from a nearby chimney. I untangled it.

Time for school. I was going to be tired. So now you know. You lucky readers.